CURSED ISLAND

WAR BETWEEN THE DEVIL AND SPIRTUAL POWERS

JEEVITA GOWD

DEDICATED TO MY MOM AND LORD

SAI DEVA WHO SHOWED THEIR

BLESSINGS ON ME FOREVER.

Contents

Contents

Foreword

THIS BOOK CONTAINS THE STORY BETWEEN
THE WAR OF EVIL SPIRITS AND SPIRITUAL POWER
.
THE ROSE WERE BORNED WITH THE
SPECIAL ABILITIES .
TO SEE THE EVIL SPIRITS THROUGH
HER VISIONS .
SHE WAS LIVING IN A ISLAND THAT
EVERY ONE WAS DISAPPEARING IN A
MYSTICAL WAY .
CAN SHE BE ABLE TO SAVE THEM ?
OR NOT .

Preface

THIS BOOK WERE INSPIRED BY MY
ONE OF THE DREAM .
WHICH I HAVE PENNED DOWN THE
THOUGHTS WHICH I FELT IT WOULD
BE MYSTICAL TO THE READERS .
THIS BOOK IS PURELY WRITTEN BY
MY IMAGINATION .
WITH AN INTENTION TO CREATE
A CREATIVE WRITING .

Acknowledgements

I WOULD LIKE TO SAY TO THANK YOU
TO MY LATE MOTHER –GOWRI DEVI .
WHO WAS ALWAYS THERE ON MY BACK AND
ANOTHER THANKS TO MY DAD AND MY PANDI
-SRI RAM
MY PANDI WHO SUPPORTED ME IN
MY DARKEST DAYS OF MY LIFE .

Prologue

THIS STORY IS HAPPENED BACK IN 1977
SOMETIMES WHEN WE GO TO THE DEPTH ALSO
WE COULD NOT FIND SOLUTION OF
SOME MYSTERIOUS THINGS WHICH ARE
ALWAYS LEFT UNSOLVED .
THIS STORY ALSO CONTAIN MANY UNSOLVED
MYSTERY OF THE WORLD .
WHICH IS OUT OF CONTROL TO THE
THOUGHT OF HUMAN .
"THERE IS A VILLAGE WITH HAPPY
SURROUNDINGS
PEOPLE ARE FILLED WITH CULTURAL JOY
AND IMMENSE JOY.
IN FEW DAYS PEOPLE IS GETTING
SUSPISIOUS .
PEOPLE WHO WENT FOR FISHING .
THE PEOPLE ARE WENT MISSING AND
NEVER CAME BACK .
THE ISLAND WHICH
WERE SURROUNDED BY THE EVIL SPIRITS.

Author Bio

INTRODUCTION OF THE AUTHOR
MEET THE AUTHOR –MISS JEEVITA GOWD
SHE COMPLETED HER BACHELOR OF
BUSINESS ADMINSTRATION .
SHE IS AN AUTHOR BY PROFESSION
AND MODEL BY PASSION.
HER HONOURS – SHE WAS THE AUTHOR OF
THE 6 BOOKS AND DID 2 ANTHALOGIES
AND WAS CO – AUTHOR OF 7 BOOKS
1- THE WAY TO SUCCESS BY ACCEPTING PAIN AND
REALITY .
2- THE BOOK OF QUOTES.
3- SUCCESS MINDSETS.
4- LOVE STORY OF ALICE AND DANID.
5-FADED DREAM OF THE PAST LIFE .
SHE WAS HONOURED WITH THE GLORY AWARD
OF INDIA AS A WRITER .
HER ACHIEVEMENTS IN MODELLING FIELD
MISS BHARAT OF CHATTISGARH 2020
MISS REPUBLIC OF CHATTISGARH
MISS REPUBLIC OF INDIA SECOND RUNNER UP
MISS BHARAT OF INDIA WINNER
MISS VIZAG RUNNER UP
SHE REPRESENTED IN INTERNATIONAL RAMP
AND DONE MANY NATIONAL LEVEL RAMPS
AND FASHION WEEKS .
SHE WAS FEATURED IN MANY MAGAZINES AND
NEWS FOR HER EXCELLENCE IN WRITING .

Author Pick

AUTHOR PICK

ONE

THE WORLD IS FULL OF MYSTERIOUS

<u>**THE WORLD IS FULL OF MYSTERIOUS**</u>
THE STORY IS HAPPENED BACK IN 1977
SOMETIMES WHEN WE GO TO THE DEPTH
ALSO WE COULD NOT FIND SOLUTION .
SOME MYSTERIOUS THINGS ARE
ALWAYS LEFT UNSOLVED .
THIS STORY ALSO CONTAIN MANY UNSOLVED
MYSTERY OF THE WORLD .
WHICH IS OUT OF CONTROL TO
THE THOUGHT OF HUMAN .
"THERE IS A VILLAGE WITH HAPPY
SURROUNDINGS
PEOPLE ARE FILLED WITH CULTURAL
JOY AND IMMENSE JOY.
IN FEW DAYS PEOPLE IS GETTING SUSPISIOUS .
PEOPLE WHO WENT FOR FISHING .

THE PEOPLE ARE WENT MISSING .
FIRST DAY THREE MEMBERS WERE MISSING SO
THE ONE WHO STAYS IN THEIR SURROUNDING
AND
FAMILY CRYING OVER FOR NOT FINDING
THE MEMBER OF HIS FAMILY.
NEXT DAY THREE MORE MEMBERS WENT TO
SEARCH
THE MISSING MEMBERS BUT MEANWHILE
THEY ALSO DISAPPEARED THE WHOLE VILLAGE
WAS SCREAMING CRYING LOUD AND SHOUTING
FOR LOOSING THEIR MEMBERS .
THAN FEW MORE MEMBERS WENT TO RESCUE
THEM BUT EVERYONE DISAPPEARED .
EVERYTHING SEEMS VERY SUSPICIOUS THEIR.
THE PEOPLE WAITED A LOT FOR THE PEOPLE
WHO LEFT BUT NO ONE RETURNED .
MANY DAYS AND YEARS PASSED BUT THE PERSON
WHO WENT MISSING DID NOT CAME BACK HOME .
VILLAGERS STARTED BELIEVING THAT GOD GAVE
CURSE
TO THEM FOR THEIR WRONG DOINGS AND FEW
PEOPLE
BELIEVED THAT WAS A GHOST ISLAND .
THEY STARTED BELIEVING .
WHOMEVER IS GOING TO THE ISLAND .
THE GHOST WAS MAKING THEM A MEAL.
PEOPLE STARTED BELIEVING MANY SAYINGS
AND STOPPED GOING TO ISLAND.

TWO

THE DAYS AFTER GETTING MISSING OF PEOPLE

—♡—

THE DAYS AFTER GETTING MISSING OF PEOPLE
THE MEMBERS OF THE VILLAGE WERE
FILLED WITH SORROW .
THE WOMENS IN THE VILLAGE HAD
CRIED ALL NIGHT .
SORROWING OVER THE MISSING PERSONS
IN THE FAMILY .
THEY WERE UNABLE TO SLEEP .
THEY FILLED WITH THE STRESS .
UNABLE TO UNDERSTAND THE REALITY .
THEY ARE NOT EVEN READY TO
ACCEPT THE TRUTH.
IT IS HARD FOR THEM TO EARN LIVELIHOOD
FOR THEIR CHILDRENS .

**WHO WERE REALLY YOUNG .
THEY ARE DEPENDED ON THEM .
THEY DOESNT EVEN BE ABLE TO UNDERSTAND
BECAUSE
THEY CANT EVEN FIND THE PERSONS WHO WENT
MISSING
OR THEY COULD NEITHER FIND THEIR BODIES**

THREE

THE PERSONS WHO ARE COMING BACK

THE PERSONS WHO ARE COMING BACK
OTHER PEOPLE WHO ARE GOING NEAR
PLACES ARE COMING BACK .
MANY PEOPLES ARE RETURNING BACK T
O THE VILLAGE AND SOME WENT MISSING .
THE OTHER VILLAGERS WHEE COMING FOR THE
FESTIVAL WHICH IS GOING TO START IN FEW
DAYS.

FOUR

GATHERING OF VILLAGERS

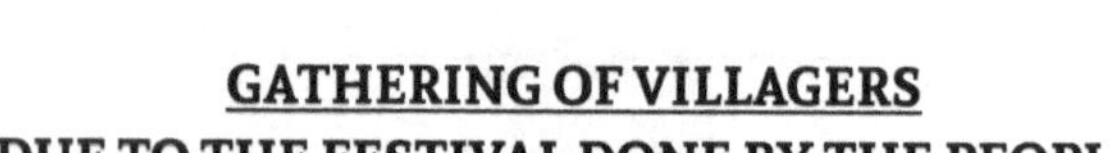

GATHERING OF VILLAGERS
DUE TO THE FESTIVAL DONE BY THE PEOPLE TO THE
MOUNTAIN GOD FROM MANY VILLAGES
PEOPLE STARTED GATHERING .
THEY WHERE BUSY WITH THE DECORATION OF
LIGHT AND ANIMALS FOR DOING RITUALS LIKE
BALI .
SACRIFISING ANIMAL TO GOD .
EVERYTHING EVERYONE IS ARRANGING
WITH WHOLE HEARTEDLY .
WOMEN AND MAN ARE PREAPARING
HAND MADE ORNAMENTS.

FIVE
RITUALS

—♡—

<u>**RITUALS**</u>
**FINALLY AFTER ALL ARRANGEMENTS .
THE NIGHT OF FESTIVAL ARRIVED .
ON THE AUSPICIOUS DAY .HAS CAME TO AN END .
EVERYONE DECORATED THEMSELVES WITH
DIFFERENT ORNAMENTS.
THEY STARTED PREAPARING FOR NIGHT RITUALS .
AT NIGHT THEY STARTED PERFORMING
RITUALS BUT AT THE SAME TIME.
THE LIGHTING WITH THE SUDDEN THUNDER.
LOUD SOUND.
ANGER SEA WITH THE HIGH WAVES .
THE SEA SEEMS LIKE ITS CURSING EVERYONE.
THE SEA WATER HIGH RAIN SPOILED
ALL ARRANGMENT.
EVERYTHING WENT TO THE VEINS.
THE PEOPLE STARTED SHOUTING
THE SUPER NATURAL POWER ARE WOKE UP.
THE MYSTERIOUS POWER CURSED US.
EVERYONE WILL DIE IN THE ISLAND
EVERYONE SHOUTED WITH HUGE VOICE WITH**

**FEAR OF DEATH AND CURSE GIVEN BY THE
POWERS.
EVERYONE STARTED TRYING TO PLEASE
THE POWERS BUT THE NATURE WAS IS
NOT CONTROL IN ANYONE'S HAND .
EVERYONE RUSHED TOWARDS THEIR HOME.
THEY WENT AND CLOSED THE DOORS AND
TRYING TO PROTECT THEMSELVES AND THEIR
FAMILIES.
THAT NIGHT EVERYONE WAS IN TROUBLE FOR .
EVERYONE WAITED FOR THE SUNRISE AND TO
SEE THE DISASTER END**

SIX

DISCUSSION OF THE MISSING PEOPLE

❦

<u>DISCUSSION OF THE MISSING PEOPLE</u>
NEXT DAY MORNING WHEN EVERYTHING
SETTLED DOWN .
FEW FAMILIES CAME OUT OF
THEIR HOME.
BY SEEING MOST OF THE PEOPLE CAME OUT.
THEY MADE A CIRCLE TYPE
AND SAT ROUND .
THEY STARTED SHARING HOW THEY
FELT AT THE TIME OF FLOOD .
SOME ANOTHER PEOPLE OUT OF
THE VILLAGE ASKED WHY THE SEA IS CLOSED.
OUT OF CURIOSITY OTHER PEOPLE ALSO ASKED
WHY THERE IS RESTICTIONS FOR TRAVELLING IN
SEA.
THEN OTHER REPLIED .

STRANGE THINGS HAPPENING
THIS DAYS. IN THE SEA .
MANY FAMILIES WHO WENT FOR FISHING
DID NOT RETURN TO THE HOME.
THEY WENT MISSING .
THEN FEW SAID WE WENT
TODAY BUT WE CAME SAFE .
THEN OTHER SUGGESTED .WHEN MALE MEMBERS
WHO ARE TRAVELLING THROUGH SEA.
WILL INFORM OTHER PEOPLE .
WHERE THEY ARE GOING .
SO THEY CAN KNOW THE SUSPICIOUS THING
BEHIND THE MISSING BUT THE PEOPLE WHO
WENT MISSING THEY DIDN'T RETURNED BACK.

SEVEN

CLOSING OF ISLAND

<u>CLOSING OF ISLAND</u>
AFTER FEW DAYS THE
PEOPLE DECIDED TO CLOSE THE
OUTGOING OF ISLAND .
ITS HARD FOR THEM TO BELIEVE
WHATS GOING IN THE SURROUNDINGS .
ITS HARD TO MAKE LIVING WITHOUT GOING OUT
BUT THE ISLAND BECOMING MORE SUSPIOUS DAY
BY DAY .
PEOPLE ARE NOT COMING BACK .THEY CANT EARN
.
ITS DIFFICULT FOR THEM BUT THEY DID.
EVERYONE DECIDED NOT TO TRAVEL THROUGH
SEA.
THEY STOPPED TAKING BOATS IN THE SEA.
THE ISLAND WAS CLOSED FOREVER.

EIGHT

THE GIRL WHO HAD FADED MEMORIES

<u>THE GIRL WHO HAD FADED MEMORIES</u>
THEIR WAS A GIRL WHO WAS RECENT BORN AND
WHEN SHE FINALLY TURN
TO SIX YEARS .
WHEN SHE WAS SMALL IN MIDDLE OF
THE NIGHT SHE USED TO CRY .
EVERYONE THOUGHT THAT THE CHILDREN
WILL CRY AT NIGHT .
SO THEY DID NOT TOOK THE BABY GIRL
TEARS SERIOUSLY .
AT THE AGE OF SIX .
ONE FINE DAY .
SHE WAS PLAYING .
HER FRIENDS GOT A MAP
WHILE PLAYING .
WHEN SHE EXPLAINED THE COMPLETE MAP

LIKE SHE WAS WELL AWARE OF IT.
SHE EXPLAINED EVERY WAY OF THE MAP.
THEN HER FRIENDS TWO BOYS STARTED
LAUGHING ON HER BUT SHE EXPLAINED LIKE
SHE KNOW EVERY CORNER OF THE MAP.
THEN THAT TWO BOYS TOOK
THAT MAP TO HIS FATHER .
THE CHILD FATHER TOOK THE MAP
AND SHOWED TO THE ELDERS OF VILLAGERS.
THEN OLD MAN SURPRISINGLY ASKED FROM
WHERE DO YOU GOT THIS PRECIOUS MAP ?
THEN HE REPLIED THEY WERE PLAYING IN THE
GROUND MEANWHILE THEY
GOT THIS AT THE SAME TIME.
THE CHILDREN WHO WERE PLAYING
THEY SAID THIS GIRL WANT TO SAY SOMETHING .
THEN OLD MAN GIVEN CHANCE TO
ROSE TO SPEAK UP WHAT SHE WANTS TO EXPRESS
.

THEN ROSE ASKED OLD MAN TO SHOW THE MAP.
THEN OLD MAN LET HER SEE THE MAP.
THEN ROSE SAID EVERYTHING IN THE MAP .
THE COMPLETE ROUTE OF THE MAP.
THE OLD MAN SHOCKED THAT HOW
SHE COULD BE ABLE TO KNOW
THE DEPTH OF THE MAP.
WHEN THERE IS NO CHANCES FOR NORMAL
PEOPLE
TO UNDERSTAND THE DEEPEST SECTRETS OF THE
MAP.
THE MAP WAS IN SECRET LANGUAGE
WHERE ONLY VERY FEW COULD UNDERSTAND .
THEN OLDMAN ASKED ROSE ?

HOW WOULD YOU KNOW ABOUT THIS MAP ROSE?
THIS IS VERY FEW PEOPLE KNOW
THE SECRET OF THE ISLAND.
THEN ROSE REPLIED I DON'T KNOW
HOW I KNOW BUT ROSE SAID I REMEMBER
CLEARLY AS I KNOW EVERYTHING.
I HAD A VISION IN MY PAST ABOUT ALL
THIS PLACES AND REMEMBER CLEARLY.
I ALSO WANT TO KNOW HOW I KNOW
ABOUT THIS BECAUSE I NEVER WENT BEFORE .

NINE

FADING MEMORIES

FADING MEMORIES
AFTER THE CONVERSATION WITH THE OLD MAN
ROSE RETURNED BACK TO THE HOME .
EVERYONE IN THE FAMILY STARTED ASKING
ROSE ABOUT HER VISIONS AND WAS CURIOUS
WHAT ELSE SHE KNEW ABOUT THE PLACES
AND HOW FAR SHE CAN BE ABLE TO REMEMBER
THE PLACES AND CAN SHE BE ABLE TO EXACTLY
EXPLAIN WHAT ELSE SHE REMEMBERS?
SHE EXPRESSED THAT SHE HAD VISIONS
ABOUT THE PLACES LIKE SHE STAYED THERE .
ROSE PARENTS WERE SHOCKED WITH HER
REPLY BECAUSE SHE IS STILL A SMALL GIRL
AND THEY NEVER TOOK ROSE
OUTSIDE OF HER ISLAND .
THEY ALL FIND VERY SUSPICIOUS
ABOUT ROSE WORDS.
AFTER SOME TIME ROSE WENT TO SLEEP .
ROSE SLEPT .

SOMEONE STARTED
CALLING HER NAME OF ROSE.
ROSE WOKEUP AND SAW EVERYWHERE
BUT NO ONE WAS THERE .
SOME STRANGE THINGS STARTED
HAPPENING WITH THE ROSE .
SOMEONE WAS CALLING HER TO OPEN
THE ISLAND WHICH WAS LOCKED FOR A LONG
TIME .
SOMEONE WAS CALLING FOR HER NAME .
SHE WOKE UP EVERYNIGHT FROM THE AGE OF SIX
YEARS .
SHE WAS BECOMING DIFFERENT FROM OTHERS .
WHEN SHE TURNED TO FIFTEEN YEARS OLD THEN
SHE TRIED TO GO TO THE CAVE
WHICH WAS CLOSE FOR THE LAST TWENTY YEARS
.
FROM WHEN SHE WAS SIX YEARS OLD .
SHE CANT EVEN SLEEP FOR A SINGLE DAY .
WHEN ROSE CLOSE HER EYES .
SHE WAS ABLE TO HEAR DIFFERENT VOICES .
ROSE STARTED GETTING
DIFFERENT IILUSIONS OF MANY PEOPLE
WHO WANT HER TO FREE THEM BUT THEY WERE
CAGED FROM SOMEONE FROM A LONG TIME .
THE PLACE WAS LOCKED .THEY WERE CALLING
FOR THE HELP .
SHE COULDNOT BE ABLE TO UNDERSTAND
WHAT IS HAPPENING WITH HER.
SHE WAS CURIOUS ABOUT EVERYTHING
HAPPENED TO HER .
WHY SHE IS THE ONLY ONE SHE IS DREAMING
WEIRD DREAMS AND HEARING TERRIFIC VOICES .

WHY SHE IS THE ONLY ONE WHO IS SUFFERING FROM THIS ALL WORSE THINGS.

TEN

ROSE MEET WITH THE FATHER

ROSE MEET WITH THE FATHER
THEN ROSE WENT TO CHURCH SHE ASKED
THE FATHER THAT WHAT IS HAPPENING WITH
HER .
ROSE EXPLAINED EVERYTHING WHICH IS
HAPPENING WITH HER AND WHAT KIND OF
DREAMS .
SHE IS BEEN DREAMING .
THEN FATHER PRAYED TO JESUS AND REPLIED
TO ROSE THAT SHE WAS BORN WITH THE
DIFFERENT PURPOSE IN THIS WORLD .
IF YOU'RE THE ONLY ONE WHO IS KEEP ON
DREAMING
ABOUT IT THEN IT IS RELATED TO YOUR
PAST LIFE OR IT IS RELATED TO YOU AND
THAT POWER NEEDS YOUR HELP.
THEN ROSE EXPLAINED THE CHILDHOOD
INCIDENT OF HER .
FATHER SAID NO MATTER WHAT HAPPENS

TO YOU JUST CLOSE YOUR EYES JESUS IS WITH
YOU .
IF YOU ARE DREAMING SOMETHING THAN IT
WANT TO CONVEY MESSAGE TO YOU .
IN THE FORM OF DREAMS.
THE REASON IT IS COMING TO YOU BECAUSE
IT NEEDS A VOICE TO BE HEARD .
FATHER SAID TO ROSE IF SOMEONE IS CALLING
FOR
YOUR HELP AND IF YOU GET TO HEAR
THE UNKNOWN VOICES DON'T NEGLECT IT.
FIND ANSWER FOR EVERY DREAM .
THEN AFTER SPEAKING WITH
FATHER ROSE FELT LITTLE BIT RELIEVED
AND SHE WALKED TOWARDS HOME.

ELEVEN

ROSE CONNECTION WITH THE PAST LIFE

—❦—

<u>ROSE CONNECTION WITH THE PAST LIFE</u>
AFTER COMING HOME ROSE REALIZED
AFTER SPEAKING WITH THE FATHER .
THAT WHAT SHE IS DREAMING THAT
MAY BE CONNECTED WITH HER PAST LIFE.
SHE WAS ANXIOUS TO KNOW THE TRUTH BEHIND
HER PAST LIFE AND THE CONNECTION BETWEEN
THE
STRANGE VOICES AND HER BUT ONE THING SHE
KNOW
THAT SHE WAS RELATED WITH THE DREAMS
SOMEHOW AND SHE DON'T KNOW HOW.
ROSE TOOK PAPERS AND INK .
SHE NOTED EVERYDREAM SHE GOT .

SHE WAS NOT SURE ABOUT VOICES BUT
SHE WAS SURE ABOUT WORDS .
SHE REMEMBERED THE WORDS .
WHICH SHE NOTED DOWN IN THE PAPERS .
FROM THAT DAY SHE WAS NOT WORRIED ABOUT
THE
DREAMS BUT SHE STARTED COLLECTING
EVERY INFORMATION AND STARTED PUTTING
DOWN ON THE PAPER.
SHE WAS SURE THAT NOT NOW BUT ONE DAY
SURELY SHE WILL FIND ANSWERS ABOUT ALL
QUESTIONS AND ANSWERS ABOUT THE DREAMS .
SHE WAS CALM AND FOCUSING ON EVERY SMALL
CLUE.
MAY BE LATE IT SEEMS TO BE BUT SHE WAS
CONFIDENT AND SHE UNDERSTOOD THAT
SHE WAS NOT A NORMAL HUMAN BEING .
SHE WAS BORN FOR A DIFFERENT PURPOSE ON
THIS EARTH .

TWELVE

ROSE DREAM

ROSE DREAM
ONE NIGHT WHEN SHE WAS TRYING
TO RECOLLECT THE MEMORIES.
SHE SUDDENLY FALLEN ASLEEP.
SHE WAS SEEING A GIRL IN HER DREAM.
WHO'S FACE WAS BLUR BUT SHE SAW
THAT GIRL WAS DOING SOME RESEARCH
ON SOME RARE MATERIALS BUT AT THE SAME
TIME .
SHE WAS SURRONDED BY FEW GANGSTERS
WHO CAME TO KILL THAT GIRL BUT SHE
RAN AWAY BUT SHE COULD NOT RUN
FURTHER THAN STILL LAST .
SHE TRIED TO ESCAPE BUT WITH THE
TERRIFIED GANGSTERS .
SHE CANT RUN OFF FOR FURTHER THAN
SHE DON'T WANT TO REVEAL THE THINGS .
SHE GOT TO KNOWN BY THE RESEARCHER
THEN SHE RAN TOWARDS THE OCEAN ROOFTOOP.
SHE JUMPED INTO THE OCEAN .
TO END HERSELF BY FALLING INTO THE

WATER RATHER THAN BEING KILLED BY THE
GANGSTERS .
ROSE SUDDENLY SCARED BY THE DREAMS AND
WOKE UP .
SHE WAS TRYING TO REMEMBER
THE THINGS BUT SHE CANNOT REMEMBER
CLEARLY .
THINGS WAS NOT EASY FOR HER .
SHE WAS HAVING A LOT OF THINGS TO
KNOW BUT SHE CANT FIND THE ANSWER OF IT.

THIRTEEN

ON THE WAY TO ABROAD

ON THE WAY TO ABROAD
ROSE GREW UP WELL.
WITH THE VARIOUS KNOWLEDGE
OVER ALL THINGS.
ROSE DECIDED TO GO ABROAD.
ROSE KNOWS SHE WAS NOT AN
ORDINARY GIRL.
TO KNOW THE MEANING OF DREAMS.
ROSE UNDERSTOOD THAT SHE CANT
FIND THE ANSWER HERE IN THE ISLAND.
SHE NEEDS TO GO TO THE ABROAD SO
SHE CAN BECOME HISTORICAL RESEARCHER
AND LEARN ABOUT SCIENCE ABOUT THE HISTORY
SO SHE CAN COME BACK .WITH THE THINGS
SHE WANTED TO KNOW.
SHE CAN UNDERSTAND SOME BASIC ABOUT
THE HISTORY AND SCIENCE SO IT WOULD BE
HELPFUL TO HER TO GET SOME HINT ON THE
PURPOSE ,

WHY SHE WAS ALIVE ?
SO SHE WENT TO ABROAD AND FOR THE
TEN YEARS SHE DISAPPEARED FROM
EVERYONE EYES AND FOCUSED ON THE
PURPOSE WHY SHE CAME TO ABROAD TO
KNOW THE FACTS BEHIND THAT WEIRD DREAMS.
SPIRITS DON'T LEAVE
EVEN AFTER CHANGING THE PLACE
THE SPIRITS DOESN'T LEFT HER .
ON EVERY RESEARCH SHE TRIED TO
DO THERE COMES TO AN END WITH
THE SUPREME POWER OF EVIL SPIRITS .
ITS NOT AN EASY TASK TO PLAY WITH
THE BAD SPIRITS .
ON EVERYSTEP SHE NEEDS TO TEST HER
LIFE TO KNOW THE TRUTH BEHIND THE THINGS .
THINGS WERE NEVER AN EASY TASK ON
HER BUT SHE TRIED TO FIND THE BEST SOLUTION
FOR THE DREAMS.

FOURTEEN

ROSE TEN YEARS IN ABROAD

ROSE TEN YEARS IN ABROAD
SHE SPENT WHOLE TEN YEARS IN
ABROAD BY LEARNING ABOUT THE
FACTS AND SCIENCE ABOUT PAST.
THEN SHE TOOK TRAINING AND
SHE DID MANY PART TIME JOBS IN RESEARCH
LABS.
FINALLY AFTER TEN YEARS SHE
DECIDED TO GO HER HOMETOWN .

FIFTEEN

RETURNING TO HOME

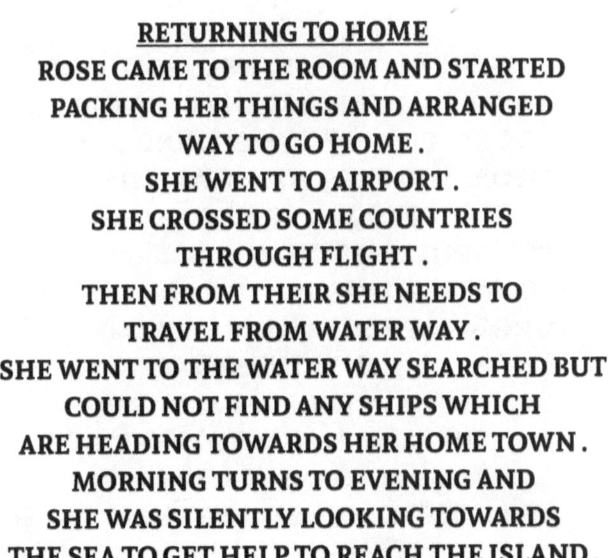

SIXTEEN

A STRANGER APPEARED

♡

A STRANGER APPEARED
THEN WITH THE SUNSET ROSE IS ABLE
TO SEE SOMEONE BUT SHE CANNOT BE ABLE
TO SEE CLEARLY .EVERYTHING WAS BLUR
BEFORE HER EYES .ROSE STARTED SHOUTING
IN A LOUD VOICE HELP ME.
PLEASE HELP ME .THEN ROSE SAW THE BOAT
IS COMING TOWARDS HER .THEN ROSE TOOK A
LONG BREATH BY FEELING RELAXED THAT SHE
CAN RETURN HOME.
THEN THE BOAT ARRIVED .
SHE SAW A MAN WHO IS HAVING A
CHARMING LOOK .
THEN BEFORE SHE SAY ANYTHING THE BOY
SAID TO COME INSIDE THE BOAT I KNEW
WHERE YOU WANT TO GO.
THEN SHE SAT ON BOAT AND WHEN SHE
SAT ON BOAT AND WHEN SHE GOT CONSICIOUS .
SHE WAS ALREADY REACHED TO ISLAND ROSE

SEARCHED EVERYWHERE FOR THAT BOY BUT
SHE COULDNOT FIND HIM. THEN ROSE STARTED
THINKING HOW SHE CAME TO THE ISLAND .
SHE CANT EVEN REMEMBER WHAT HAPPENED
AND WHY SHE CANT REMEMBER HIS FACE .
EVERYTHING HAPPENING WITH THE ROSE WAS
LIKE A MIRACLE OR A CURSE SHE WAS NOT
AWARE OF IT .
SHE COULDNOT UNDERSTAND WHAT IS
HAPPENING .

SEVENTEEN
EMPTY ISLAND

<u>EMPTY ISLAND</u>
WHEN ROSE STARTED SEARCHING
SHE COULDNOT FIND EVEN FEW PEOPLE IN
ISLAND .
SHE WAS SCARED A LOT.SHE WENT TO
CHECK ON THE HOUSES BUT SHE COULDNOT
BE ABLE TO FIND PEOPLE.
THEN AFTER A LONG TIME SHE SAW SOME PEOPLE
.

ROSE STARTED ASKING QUESTIONS WITH SO
MUCH PEOPLE .SHE WAS CURIOUS AND SCARED .
THEN THE REMANING FAMILY WHO LEFT OVER
THE ISLAND REPLIED THAT ALL THE FAMILIES
DISAPPEARED SUDDENLY AND THEY NEVER CAME
BACK
AND THE PEOPLE WHO CAME BACK THEY DON'T
HAVE
ANY MEMORIES ABOUT WHAT ACTUALLY
HAPPENED
TO THEM IN THE PAST .FOR ROSE THAT WAS NOT A

SURPRISE BECAUSE FROM CHILDHOOD SHE SAW MANY
THINGS WHICH SCIENCE CANNOT ANSWER SO ROSE
DECIDED TO CHECK FURTHER DETAILS ABOUT THE ISLAND .
SHE WENT TO HOUSE BUT SHE CANNOT FIND HER
PARENTS IN HOME .SHE WAS SCARED LIKE ANYTHING .
SHE WAS BROKEN .ROSE STARTED CRYING .
SHE DIDN'T EVEN NOTICED THAT SOMEONE
IS KNOCKING THE DOOR .
SHE WENT AND OPENED THE DOOR .SHE SAW A BOY .
THEN SHE ASKED ?WHO ARE YOU?THEN HE REPLIED
I AM HERE TO SAY YOU SOMETHING .
THEN ROSE SAID OK PLEASE GO AHEAD SAY WHAT
YOU WANT TO EXPRESS .THEN HE SAID IF YOU
ARE TRYING TO SAVE EVERYBODY THEN YOU WONT
BE ALIVE IN THIS ISLAND HAS BEEN CURSED.
SO STOP CRYING AND TRY TO FIND THE ANSWER
WITHOUT GIVING UP ON YOUR LIFE AND DISAPPEARED.
ROSE WAS LIKE SHE DON'T UNDERSTAND
WHO HE WAS BUT ONE THING .
SHE UNDERTSTOOD THAT SHE IS SPECIAL
AND SHE NEEDS TO KNOW THE MYSTERY OF
HER LIFE AND NEED TO UNDERSTAND THE DEPTH
OF HER ANSWERS OF THE MYSTERY BEHIND.
WHEN SHE THOUGHT TO SLEEP THEN THE SAME BOY

APPEARED IN THE DREAM WHEN SHE WAS ALONE
AND CRYING.
HE JUST HOLDED HER HAND AND SAID DON'T
WORRY
THIS WILL PASS BY.DONT CRY YOUR FAMILY IS
SAFE JUST
THEY MOVED TO ANOTHER VILLAGE .
YOUR SPECIAL ROSE BUT DON'T RISK YOUR LIFE.
I WILL SOON MEET YOU .
SUDDENLY SHE WOKE UP FROM THE DREAM .
SHE SEARCHED EVERYWHERE BUT SHE
COULDNOT
BE ABLE TO FIND THE BOY .
SHE ALWAYS GET WEIRD DREAMS BUT FOR THE
FIRST
TIME WHEN SHE WOKE UP FROM HER DREAM.
SHE HAD TEARS ON HER FACE .WITH THE LOVE
SHE FEELS SO WORSE FOR NOT BE ABLE TO
REMEMBER
HIS FACE .
SHE STARTED THINKING OF THE BOY.
SHE DREAMT OF AND THE ONE WHO
DISAPPEARED
WHO WAS ALIVE IN THE ISLAND AND WHY
HE IS SAYING HER TO GO AWAY FROM THIS
ISLAND .
WHAT IS HIS PURPOSE TO SEE ME AND HOW HE
CAN DISAPPEAR SUDDENLY .
WHILE THINKING SHE SLEPT .
SHE AGAIN GOT WEIRD DREAM LIKE SHE
ALWAYS USED TO GET BUT SHE REMEMBER
THAT WHEN SHE IS IN ABROAD SHE DIDN'T
HAD ANY DREAM BUT SOMEWHERE SHE WAS

HAPPY THAT HER FAMILY WAS ALIVE .
SHE CAME UP WITH A PLAN
THEN WHOLE NIGHT SHE THOUGHT OF
A PLAN AND IN THE MORNING SHE WANT TO
EXCUTE IT .
AS THE WAY SHE THOUGHT SHE GATHERED
NUMBERS OF MANY REASEARCHERS AND
SCIENTISTS AS PER SHE CAN GATHER.
THEN SHE CONTACTED MANY PEOPLE BUT
FEW WERE AGREED TO IT .
SOME REJECTED IT BECAUSE THIS WAS A
DANGEROUS ISLAND AND SOME SCIENTISTS
THIS TOOK THIS AS A CHALLENGE AND THEN
AGREED PEOPLE STARTED THEIR JOURNEY
TOWARDS ISLAND.

EIGHTEEN

THE JOURNEY TOWARDS ISLAND

THE JOURNEY TOWARDS ISLAND
COMPLETE 30 PEOPLE DECIDED TO START
JOURNEY TOWARDS ISLAND .IN THAT TEN
WERE TOP SCIENTIST AND FIVE WERE INTERNS
AND REMANING PEOPLE WERE REASEARCHERS
ABOUT HISTORY AND MYSTERICAL FACTS AND
SOME NEWS CHANNELS ALSO WANT TO JOIN TO
GET SOME DIFFERENT NEWS .
THEY ARRANGED ALL EQUIPMENTS TO COLLECT
PROOFS AND STARTED JOURNEY TOWARDS
ISLAND.
THEY CAME TO THE ISLAND WAITING TO TRAVEL
FROM WATERWAY BUT THEY NEED BOAT OR SHIP
FROM WHICH THEY CAN TRAVEL BUT
UNFOURTUNETELY .

THEY WAITED FROM THE MORNING TILL
EVENING THEY
CANNOT FIND A SINGLE BOAT .
THEY THOUGHT TO GIVE UP
AND RETURN AT THE SAME TIME .FROM DISTANCE
THEY
SAW A WOMEN IN THE BOAT SHE IS COMING TO
THEIR SIDE .
THEY STARTED SHOUTING IN A LOUD VOICE FOR
HER TO HELP .
THEN THE LADY SUDDENLY APPEARED WITHOUT
TAKING ANY TIME.
THEY ALL WERE SHOCKED THAT THEY SAW HER
VERY FAR WITHIN BLINK OF THE EYE .
SHE WAS IN FRONT OF THEM .
ALL PEOPLE ASKED
WOMEN IF SHE CAN TAKE THEM ALL TO THE
ISLAND .
THEN WITH A LOUD VOICE SHE SHOUTED
IF WANT TO LIVE GO BACK TO YOUR PLACES OR
EVEN PEOPLE CANT FIND YOUR DEAD BODY .
THEN FEW PEOPLE ASKED WHY ARE YOU SAYING
LIKE THIS .
THEN SHE REPLIED THAT ISLAND IS IN THE
POWER OF SPIRITS .
WITHOUT SPIRIT PERMISSION YOU CANNOT GO
TO THE ISLAND .
THEN SCIENTIST LAUGHED AND SAID SPIRITS
DON'T EXISTS AND STARTED LAUGHING AND SAID
IF YOU CAN TAKE US THERE TAKE OR JUST LEAVE
US HERE .
THEN SHE LAUGHED BY FEELING PITY ON THEM .

NINETEEN

A MYSTERIOUS NIGHT

A MYSTERIOUS NIGHT
THEY WERE LEFT IN THE PLACE BY NOT
HAVING ANY MEANS WHICH THEY CAN
TRAVEL TO THE ISLAND .
SUDDENLY WITHOUT THEIR CONSIOUS
WHEN THIS PEOPLE CAME TO <u>CONSIOUS</u>
THE SUN RAISED .
EVERYONE WAS SHOCKED WHEN THEY CAME
TO KNOW THEY ALREADY REACHED ISLAND
AND ATLEAST NOT EVEN A SINGLE PERSON
REMEMBER WHAT HAPPENED .
THEY CANT EVEN <u>MEMORIZE</u> HOW THEY
REACHED HERE AND EVERY PERSON WERE
SCATTERED .
THE FEW PEOPLE WHO GOT CONSICIOUS WENT
TO
SEARCH ALL PEOPLE AND THEY ALL GATHERED .
THEY FOUND EVERYONE BUT THEY CANT FIND
THE P

EOPLE FROM MEDIA. THEY WENT MISSING .
THEN ALL HISTORIANS AND <u>SCIENTISTS</u> .WERE SURPRISED
THAT IN COMPLETE TWENTY PEOPLE NOT
EVEN A SINGLE PERSON REMEMBER HOW THEY HAVE
REACHED ISLAND .
THAT BECOME MORE MYSTERIOUS THINGS TO THEM
BECAUSE NOT EVEN A SINGLE PERSON KNOWS HOW
TO GO BACK TO THEIR HOME TOWNS .
THEN THEY DECIDED TO LOOK FOR THE ROSE AND
EVERYONE GROUPED AND STARTED SEARCHING ROSE
IN DIFFERENT ROUTES AND DECIDED TO MEET ON
THE SAME SPOT AFTER TWO HOURS .
EVERYONE WENT FOR THE DIFFERENT PLACES .
THEN LASTLY THEY FOUND ROSE AND THEY CAME
BACK ALONG WITH ROSE .
EVERYONE GATHERED AT THE SAME SPOT AFTER
TWO HOURS .
EVERYONE GATHERED AT THE SAME SPOT AS
LIKE THE DISCUSSED .
AT CORRECT 6PM WHOLE LIGHTS IN THE VILLAGE
TURNED OFF AND EVERYTHING BECAME SO DARK.
THE SCIENTISTS FOUND IT IS INTRESTING BECAUSE
EVERYTHING THEY SAW IT WAS A TOPIC WHICH
SCIENCE AND HUMANS CANNOT DEAL WITH IT
EVERYTHING WAS BEYOND THE HUMAN
IMAGINATION .

WHERE SCIENCE DOESNOT HAVE ANY
EXPLANATION .
THEY EXPERINCED SCIENTISTS WERE THRILLED
OUT
TO FIND THE UNKNOWN MYSTERY BEHIND THIS
ISLAND
BUT NEWLY JOINED PEOPLE WERE LITTLE BIT
SCARED
BECAUSE THIS WAS OUT OF THEIR
IMAGINATIONS.
THEN EVERYONE WAS TIRED .
THEY MADE TENTS FOR
THEIR STAY AND RESTED FOR THAT NIGHT .
WITH THE SUN RISE EVERYONE COME OUT AND W
ANTED TO MAKE A PLAN TO SOLVE THIS MYSTERY
.
EVERYONE STARTED DISCUSSING ABOUT HOW
THEY
REACHED ISLAND BUT NO ONE CAN BE ABLE TO
REMEMBER THAT HOW THEY REACHED HERE BUT
WHAT IS THE STRANGE THING IS WHOLEDAY
HAVE
BEEN PASSED NOT EVEN A SINGLE PERSON .
KNOW HOW TO GO BACK AND WHAT HAPPENED
IN THIS MEANWHILE .

TWENTY
MAKING PLANS

<u>**MAKING PLANS**</u>
SO EVERYONE TEAMED UP TO KNOW
THE TRUTH .
EVERYONE STARTED MAKING PLANS TO
SOLVE THE HIDDEN MYSTERY BEHIND THE
CLUMSY SITUATIONS .PEOPLE TEAMED UP AND
DIVIDED INTO GROUPS.
SOME PEOPLE WAS TRYING TO ARRANGE
ALL TECHINCAL WORK AND SOME STARTED
DOING REASEARCH ON THE ISLAND .
HOW IT HAS BEEN STARTED .
HOW MANY PEOPLE DISAPPAERED .
THEY FOUND IT AS ANOTHER MYSTERY
THAT AMONG ALL FAMILIES .
IN EVERY FAMILY ONLY SINGLE
PERSON DISAPPEARED.
SOME FAMILIES REMEMBER THEIR FAMILY
MEMBER AND SOME PEOPLE TOTALLY FORGET
AND THEY WERE IN AN ILLUSION ABOUT
THE OTHER MISSING PERSON.
SOME UNKNOWN ANSWERS WITH EVERY

FAMILY THEY ASKED FOR THEY NOTED IT. EVERYONE WERE ENTANGLIED WITH THE SITUATION.

TWENTY-ONE
EXPERIMENTS

<u>**EXPERIMENTS**</u>
EXPERIMENTS AND WAYS TO GO THE ISLAND.
FIRST THE SCIENTIST TRIED TO PREPARE A BOAT
CONTAINING WITH THE VIDEO RECORDING
CAMERA
EVERYTHING WENT WELL THE CAMERA WAS
WORKING
WELL BUT WITH ALL OF SUDDEN.
WHEN THE BOAT REACHED TO THE ISLAND.
ALL CAMERA TURNED OFF.
EVERYONE PLAN WERE FAILED.
SCIENTIST GOT UPSET AND TRIED MANY WAYS
BUT AT LAST EVERYTHING FAILED.
THEY FOCUSED ON NATURAL TRIAL SCENCE FOR
THE PRESENCE OF MYSTERY.
THEY MAINLY FOCUSED ON THE IMAGES WHICH
CAN BE CAPTURED AND THE MAIN INTEREST ON
THE EVENTS HAPPENED IN THE PAST.
THEY STARTED SEARCHING FOR A SOLUTION.
HOW PEOPLE GOT DISAPPEARED.
WHY THEY COMMITED SUCIDE?

**WHY THE PEOPLE DON'T REMEMBER
ANYTHING IN THE ISLAND.
AFTER TRYING ALL METHODS THEY FAILED IN
EVERY ASPECTS .
SO FINALLY THEY DECIDED TO GO THE ISLAND.
THEY WERE PREPARING TO GO AN OLD LADY
APPEARED AND GAVE A MAGICAL STONE TO THE
ROSE AND SAID DONNOT OPEN IT WHATEVER
THE SITUATION MAY BE .
THEN ROSE SMILED AND ACCEPTED THE STONE
BEFORE SHE ASKS ANYTHING TO THE OLD LADY .
SHE DISAPPEARED IN THE MYSTICAL WAY.**

TWENTY-TWO

STARTED JOURNEY TOWARDS THE ISLAND

STARTED JOURNEY TOWARDS THE ISLAND
AFTER A LONG TRIAL THE TWENTY MEMBERS
DECIDED
TO DIRECTLY FACE AND DARED TO GO THERE .
THE SHIP WAS READY BUT NO ONE WAS THEIR
WHO
CAN TAKE THEM TO THE ISLAND .
THE TIME OF SUNSET A BOY SHOWN UP .
ALL MEMBERS ASKED HELP TO TAKE EVERYONE
TO THE ISLAND .
THEN THAT BOY WARNED IF YOU GO THERE YOU
COULDNOT RETURN BACK ALIVE BUT THEY
STILL SAID THEY CAN SOLVE ALL THE PUZZLES
AND REACH THE DESTINATION OF THE ISLAND .

TWENTY-THREE

JOURNEY STARTED

**JOURNEY STARTED
THE TWENTY MEMBERS JOURNEY
STARTED TO THE CURSED ISLAND .
WHERE NO ONE KNOWS WHAT WILL
HAPPEN NEXT BUT STARTED THE JOURNEY
WITH THE HOPE TO SOLVE ALL THE PUZZLES .**

TWENTY-FOUR
STAGES OF THE JOURNEY

STAGES OF THE JOURNEY
WHEN THE JOURNEY STARTED EVERYTHING
LOOKS SO NORMAL .
WHEN THE SHIP STARTED MOVING .
THE SHIP WAS LIFTED A BIT IN THE AIR
PEOPLE WHO WERE TRAVELLING IT WAS SO
SCARY FOR THEM .
THE SHIP WAS FLYING IN THE SKY .
IN SEA THEIR WAS DIFFERENT SPECIES .
WHICH WAS SO SCARY AND HAUNTED .
IN MEANWHILE A FLYING LIZARD CAME AND
TOOK FOUR PEOPLE .
THE REMAINING SIXTEEN PEOPLE CONDITION
WAS DEPRESSED BECAUSE FOR A MOMENT
THEY DON'T UNDERSTAND .WHAT IS HAPPENING .
THEY ARE SEEING THE THINGS WHICH
DON'T EXIST IN THE WORLD .
THEN SUDDENLY THE SKY TURNED TO RED AND
MANY DEAD SOULS WERE WANDERING AROUND

TO KILL HUMANS SOULS .
THE BOY WHO WAS TAKING CARE OF THE SHIP
DISAPPEARED .
THEN THE SHIP DISAPPEARED THERE WAS LIKE
AN OLD CAVE .
THERE WAS NO OPTIONS LEFT FOR
THE SIXTEEN REMAINING PEOPLE TO CHECK
THE CAVE THEY STICKED IN A PLACE WHERE
THEY CANT GO BACK.
THEY STARTED MOVING INSIDE THE CAVE .
THE PLACED FILLED WITH BLOOD AND BONES .
FILLED WITH UNKNOWN SPECIES WHO
WERE EATING BLOOD .
EVERYONE WAS SO SCARED BUT THEY ARE GOING .
WHEN THEY OPENED DOOR .
THE DEAD SOUL TOOK SIX PERSONS AND
KILLED THEM .
THE REMAINING TEN SCIENTISTS WERE
STARTLED .
EVEN THE REMANING SCIENTIST WERE
SCARTTERED INTO DIFFERENT LOCATION .
THE CAVE FILLED WITH THE FLESH MEAT AND
SKELTONS OF HUMANS WAS THE ONLY THING
WHICH WAS THERE IN THE ISLAND .
WHERE THEY WERE WALKING ALL
REASEARCHERS LOST THEIR LIFE IN
THE HANDS OF MYSTERY OF DEVLISH POWERS .

TWENTY-FIVE

THE POWER OF SPIRITS

THE POWER OF SPIRITS
ONLY ROSE WERE LEFT .
NO EVILS POWER COULD TOUCH
THE ROSE .
THEN ROSE REALISED SHE HAD
THE STONE MYSTICAL CHAIN IN HER NECK.
THE REASON NOTHING CAN BE ABLE TO
TOUCH ROSE .
SHE TOOK THE CHAIN AND HOLDED
WITH HER HANDS AND STARTED RUNNING .
THEN SUDDENLY SHE THOUGHT OF
THE BOY WHO DISAPPEARED .
THEN BY MISTAKEN THE STONE IN ROSE HAND
TOUCHED TO CAVE GOT BROKEN INTO TWO
PIECES .
ROSE RUNNED AWAY FROM THE CAVE .
SHE RAN OUT AND THEN SHE FOUND A WAY TO
SEE THE SPIRITUAL ISLAND FILLED WITH
POSITIVE

POWER BUT BEFORE SHE REACHES THEIR THE
STONE FALLEN DOWN AND ROSE THOUGHTS IT
WAS ENDED .
THE MYSTERY NEVER ENDED THEIR .
THE ISLAND REMAINED MYSTERIOUS FOREVER
BUT
WITHOUT KNOWING THE SPIRTUAL POWER
BROKEN
THE RULE HOLDED THE HAND OF ROSE WENT
AGAINST EVERYTHING AND SAVED HER .
BECAUSE ROSE WERE CREATED FOR THE REASON
TO FREE THE EVIL SOULS WHICH HAVE BEEN
CAGED THERE .
AFTER WAKING UP THE SPIRTUAL GOD OF CURSE.

TWENTY-SIX

AWAKENING OF THE SPIRITS

AWAKENING OF THE SPIRITS
HER WOUNDS WERE CURED BY THE POWERS
WHICH WAS LIVING THERE AND SAVED HER
THEN SHE ASKED WHY I AM THE ONLY ONE
. WHO WAS ALIVE ?THEY REPLIED YOU WERE
BORN TO GIVE THEM A NEW START .
WHO LOST THEIR LIFE IN THIS CURSED ISLAND .
THEN AGAIN SHE RISKED HER LIFE WENT TO
EVIL SOULS AND SHE STARTED DOING MANTRAS.
THE MANTRAS WHICH HAS THE POWER TO
VANISH
THE POWER OF CURSE AND CAN BE ABLE TO FREE
THEM.
THE EVILS SOULS BECOME A BEAUTIFUL SOUL
WITH THE TOUCH OF ROSE .
THEY BECAME BEAUTIFULL BUTTERFLIES
AND FLEW AWAY .

TWENTY-SEVEN
LIVED HAPPILY

<u>LIVED HAPPILY</u>
THEN THE ISLAND REMAINED WITH THE
SPIRTUAL GOD .
EVIL POWERS WHERE FREE AND HAPPY AND
MADE EVERYONE TO LEAVE THE ISLAND .
THEY CAN CURE PEOPLE BUT THEY CANT
TAKE OUT REALITY THAT THE ISLAND HAS
BEEN CURSED SO EVERYONE WAS HAPPY
THAT EVERY LOST PERSON GOT THEIR
FAMILIES BACK AND THE ISLAND DOESN'T
CONTAIN EVIL SPIRITS ANYMORE BUT
RESPECTING THE WORDS OF SPIRTUAL POWERS
THEY LEFT THE ISLAND AND LIVED
HAPPILY FOREVER ..